THE GREAT AUDITION SOURC

SECTION 1
R&B ANTHEMS

SECTION 2
ROCK CLASSICS

SECTION 3
CLASSICAL GREATS

SECTION 4
ANGELS...
PLUS 9 MORE HIT SONGS

Wise Publications
part of The Music Sales Group
London/New York/Paris/Sydney/Copenhagen/Berlin/Madrid/Tokyo

Published by
Wise Publications
14-15 Berners Street,
London W1T 3LJ, UK.

Exclusive Distributors:
Music Sales Limited
Distribution Centre, Newmarket Road,
Bury St Edmunds, Suffolk IP33 3YB, UK.
Music Sales Pty Limited
20 Resolution Drive,
Caringbah, NSW 2229, Australia.

Order No. AM995467
ISBN 978-1-84772-737-4
This book © Copyright 2008 by Wise Publications

Compiled by Nick Crispin.
Music arranged by Paul Honey.
Music processed by Paul Ewers Music Design.

CD recorded, mixed and mastered by John Rose.
Backing tracks arranged by Paul Honey.
Keyboards by Paul Honey.
Bass by Don Williams.
Drums by Brett Morgan.
Backing vocals by Alison Symons, Alexander Troy & JonasT.

Printed in the United Kingdom by
Caligraving Limited, Thetford, Norfolk.

Previously published as *Audition Songs for Males Singers R&B Anthems,*
Audition Songs for Males Singers Rock Classics,
Audition Songs for Males Singers Classical Greats &
Audition Songs for Males Singers 3: Angels...

Your Guarantee of Quality
As publishers, we strive to produce every book
to the highest commercial standards.
The music has been freshly engraved and the book has been
carefully designed to minimise awkward page turns and
to make playing from it a real pleasure.
Particular care has been given to specifying acid-free,
neutral-sized paper made from pulps which have not been
elemental chlorine bleached. This pulp is from farmed sustainable
forests and was produced with special regard for the environment.
Throughout, the printing and binding have been planned to ensure a
sturdy, attractive publication which should give years of enjoyment.
If your copy fails to meet our high standards, please inform us and
we will gladly replace it.

www.musicsales.com

SECTION 1
R&B ANTHEMS

See page 64 for full CD track listing details

Brown Sugar

Words & Music by Ali Jones-Muhammad & Michael Archer

4

Frontin'

Words by Chad Hugo, Pharrell Williams & Shawn Carter
Music by Chad Hugo & Pharrell Williams

Hey Ya!

Words & Music by André Benjamin

Hot In Herre

Words & Music by Charles Brown, Pharrell Williams & Cornell Haynes

good gra - cious, ass__ is bo - da - cious, flir - ta - cious, tryin'_ to show fa - ces.
2. Why you at the bar if you ain't poppin' the bottles? What good is all the fame if you ain't fuckin' the models? I see you

Look - in' for the right time to shoot my steam, look - in' for the right time to flash them Gs. Then, um,
drivin', sportscar, ain't hittin' the throttle and I be down, and do a hundred, top down and goggles. Get off the

I'm leav - ing, please be - liev - in' me and the rest__ of my hea - thens.
free - way, ex - it one - oh - six and parked it, ash - tray flip gate, time to spark it.

Kiss

Words & Music by Prince

1. You don't have to be beau-ti-ful to turn me on.
2. You got to not talk dirty baby if you wanna im-press me,
(3.) girls rule my world, I said, they rule my world,

I just need your you can't be too Act your

bo - dy, ba - by, from dusk till dawn.__
flirty Mam - ma, I know how to undress__ me.__
age Mam - ma, not your shoe size may - be we could do__ the twirl.

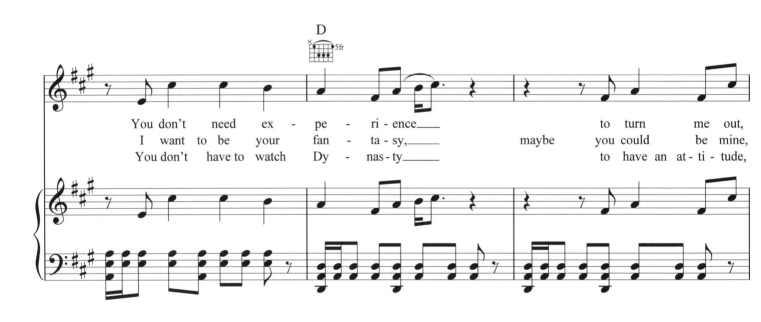

D

You don't need ex - pe - ri - ence__ to turn me out,
I want to be your fan - ta - sy,__ maybe you could be mine,
You don't have to watch Dy - nas - ty__ to have an at - ti - tude,

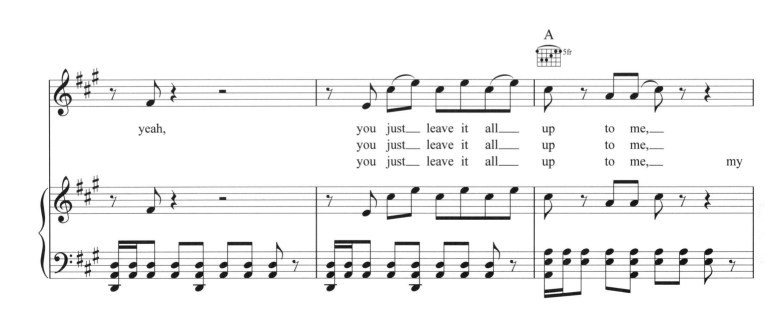

A

yeah,
you just__ leave it all__ up to me,__
you just__ leave it all__ up to me,__
you just__ leave it all__ up to me,__ my

Like I Love You

Words & Music by Pharrell Williams, Charles Hugo, Gene Thornton, Terence Thornton & Justin Timberlake

Ma, what you wanna do?
I'm in front of you.
Grab a friend, see, I can have fun with two.
Or me and you put on a stage show
And the mall kids, that's how to change low.
From them you heard "Wow, it's the same glow."
Went to me, I say, "Yeah, it's the same dough."
We the same type, you my air of life,
You have sleepin' in the same bed, any night

Girl, rock with me, you deserves the best,
Take a few shots,
Let it burn in your chest.
We could ride down
Pumpin' N.E.R.D. in the deck,
Funny how a few words turn into sex.
Play this free, joint called brain.
Ma, take a hint,
Make me swerve in the lane.
The name Malicious
And I burn every track,
Clipse and J. Timberlake,
Now, how heavy is that?

No Diggity

Words & Music by Teddy Riley, Bill Withers, Chauncey Hannibal, Lynise Walters, William Stewart & Richard Vick

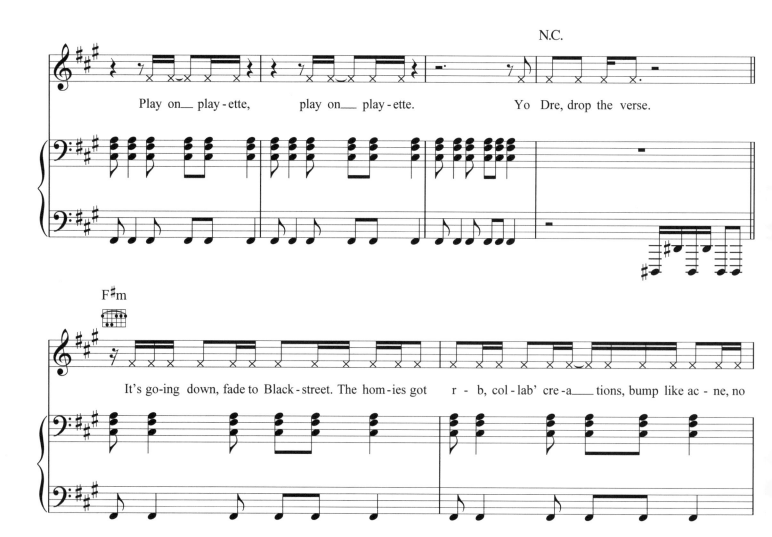

N.C.

doubt. I put it down, nev-er slouch, as long as my cre - dit can vouch, a dog could-n't catch me say-ing, "Ouch." Tell me,

F#m

who can stop when Dre mak-ing moves at- tract-ing ho-neys like a mag-net, giv-ing them ear-ga-sms with my mel-low ac-

N.C.

- cent? Still mov-ing this fla-vour with the hom-ies Black street and Ted-dy, the o-ri-gi-nal rump-sha-kers.

1. Shor- ty

F#m

in down,___ good lord,___ ba - by got 'em o - pen all ov - er town.___

(Queen Pen)
'Cos that's my peeps and we row G,
Flying first class from New York City to Blackstreet.
What you know about me? Not a motherf... thing,
Cartier, wooded frames sported by my shortie.
As for me, icy gleaming pinky diamond ring,
We be's the baddest clique up on the scene.
Ain't you getting bored with these fake-ass broads?
I shows and proves, no doubt, I be takin' you, so,
Please excuse if I come across rude,
That's just me and that's how a playette's got to be.
Stay kicking game with a capital G,
Ask the peoples on my block, I'm as real as can be.
Word is bond, faking moves never been my thing,
So, Teddy, pass the word to your nigga chauncy,
I be sitting in a car, let's say, around 3:30,
Queen Pen and Blackstreet, it's no diggity.

Rock With You

Words & Music by Rod Temperton

1. Girl,___ close your eyes, let that rhy-thm get in - to you.
2. Out on the floor there ain't no-bo-dy there but us.

She's Got That Vibe

Words & Music by R Kelly & Barry Hankerson

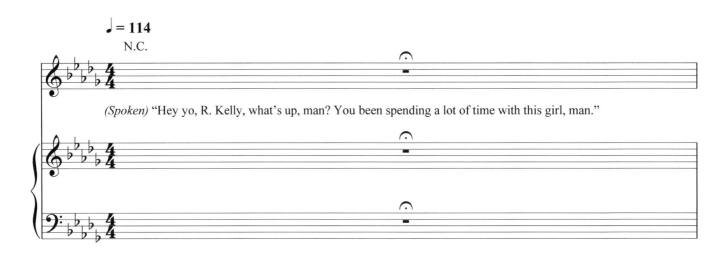

Yeah!

Words & Music by Garrett Hamler, Patrick Smith, James Phillips, Christopher Bridges, LaMarquis Jefferson, Jonathan Smith & Robert McDowell

(Spoken) Yeah! (Yeah!)   OK! (OK!)   Ush-er. (Ush-er.)   Yeah_ yeah_ yeah_ yeah_

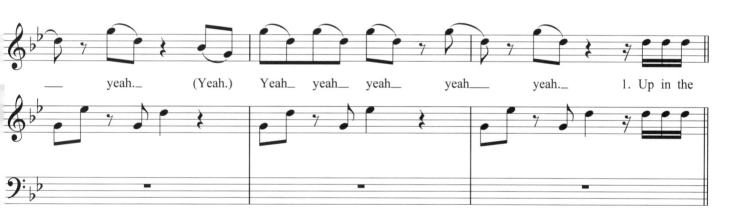

_ yeah._   (Yeah.)   Yeah_ yeah_ yeah_ yeah_ yeah._   1. Up in the

club with my ho - mies   tryin' to get a lit - tle V.   I.   but down on a low key,
(2.) all up in my head now,   got me think - in' that it might   be a good idea to take her   with me,

'cos you know how I feel._____ I saw the shor - ty she was
'cos she's rea - dy to leave._____ Then I

check - in' up on me, from the game she was spit - tin' in my ear, you would think that she knew me,
got - ta keep it real now, 'cos on a one___ to ten___ she's a cer - ti - fied___ twen - ty,

knew me, de - ci - ded to chill._____ Con - ver - sa - tion got
_____ but that just ain't me._____ 'Cos I

hea - vy,___ she had me feel - in' like she's rea - dy to blow.___ Oh.
don't_ know if I take that chance just where's it gon - na lead, but what I do know is the way she dance makes

she was all up on me scream-ing. Yeah_ yeah_ yeah_ yeah__ yeah._ (Yeah.)

To Coda ⊕ | 1. | 2.

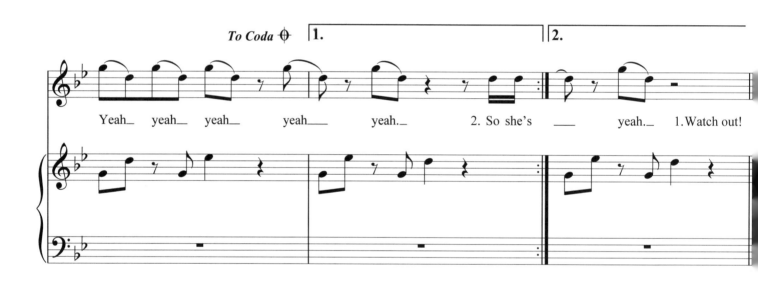

Yeah_ yeah_ yeah_ yeah__ yeah._ 2. So she's __ yeah._ 1. Watch out!

My out-fit's so rid-i-cu-lous, in the club look-in' so con-spi-cu-ous. And
2. For-get about game, I'm-a spit the truth, I won't stop un-til I get 'em in they're birth-day suit.
3. I left the Jag and took the Rolls, if they ain't cut-tin' then I put 'em on foot pa-trol.
4. Let's drink, you the one to please, Lu-da-cris fills cups like dou-ble D's. Me and

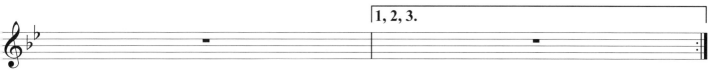

1, 2, 3.

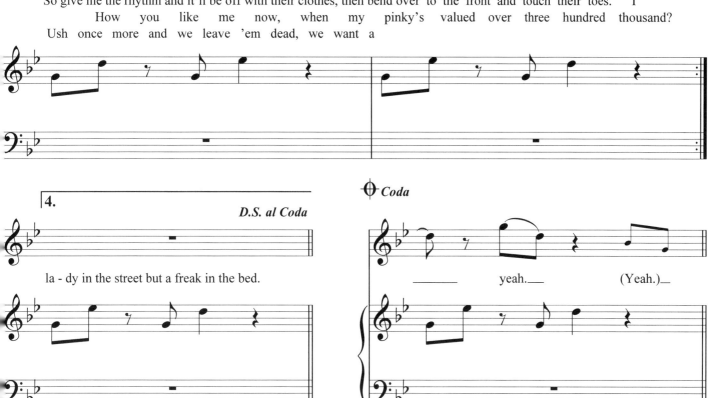

Rowl! These women all on the prowl, if you hold the head steady I'm a milk the cow.
So give me the rhythm and it'll be off with their clothes, then bend over to the front and touch their toes.   I
How you like me now, when my pinky's valued over three hundred thousand?
Ush once more and we leave 'em dead, we want a

4.

D.S. al Coda

la - dy in the street but a freak in the bed.

Coda

_____ yeah.___   (Yeah.)___

Play 4 times

1. Take that and re-wind it back,   L'il   Jon   got the beat to make ya boo-ty go.
2. Take the and re-wind it back,   Ush - er   got the voice to make ya boo-ty go.
3. Take that and re-wind it back,   Lu-da - cris   got the flow to make ya boo-ty go.
4. Take that and re-wind it back,   L'il   Jon   got the beat to make ya boo-ty go.

1 2 3 4 5 6 7 8 9

63

CD Track Listing

CD Track 1
Brown Sugar
Music: Page 2
(JONES-MUHAMMAD/ARCHER)
UNIVERSAL MUSIC PUBLISHING LIMITED/ZOMBA MUSIC PUBLISHERS LIMITED

CD Track 2
Frontin'
Music: Page 7
(HUGO/WILLIAMS/CARTER)
EMI MUSIC PUBLISHING LIMITED/BMG MUSIC PUBLISHING LIMITED

CD Track 3
Hey Ya!
Music: Page 12
(BENJAMIN) CHRYSALIS MUSIC LIMITED

CD Track 4
Hot In Herre
Music: Page 20
(BROWN/WILLIAMS/HAYNES)
EMI MUSIC PUBLISHING LIMITED/BMG MUSIC PUBLISHING LIMITED/BUG MUSIC LIMITED

CD Track 5
Kiss
Music: Page 27
(PRINCE) UNIVERSAL/MCA MUSIC LIMITED

CD Track 6
Like I Love You
Music: Page 32
(WILLIAMS/HUGO/THORNTON/THORNTON/TIMBERLAKE)
EMI MUSIC PUBLISHING LIMITED/ZOMBA MUSIC PUBLISHERS LIMITED

CD Track 7
No Diggity
Music: Page 38
(RILEY/WITHERS/HANNIBAL/WALTERS/STEWART/VICK)
ZOMBA MUSIC PUBLISHERS LIMITED/NON MEMBER/I Q MUSIC LIMITED/UNIVERSAL/
MCA MUSIC LIMITED/NOTTING HILL MUSIC (UK) LIMITED/COPYRIGHT CONTROL

CD Track 8
Rock With You
Music: Page 46
(TEMPERTON) RONDOR MUSIC (LONDON) LIMITED

CD Track 9
She's Got That Vibe
Music: Page 52
(KELLY/HANKERSON) ZOMBA MUSIC PUBLISHING LIMITED

CD Track 10
Yeah!
Music: Page 59
(HAMLER/SMITH/PHILLIPS/BRIDGES/JEFFERSON/SMITH/MCDOWELL)
EMI MUSIC PUBLISHING LIMITED/WINDSWEPT MUSIC (LONDON) LIMITED/
BUG MUSIC LIMITED/TVT MUSIC LIMITED

To remove your CD from the plastic sleeve,
lift the small lip to break the perforations.
Replace the disc after use for convenient storage.

SECTION 2
ROCK CLASSICS

20th Century Boy

Words & Music by Marc Bolan

(Aah.)

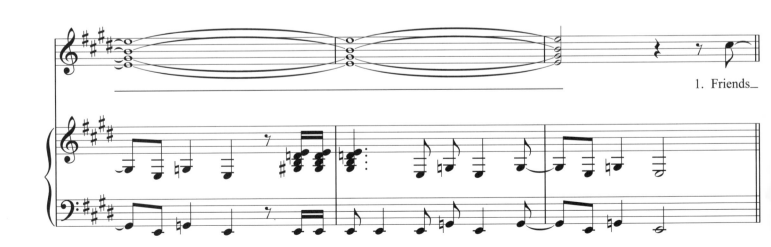

1. Friends

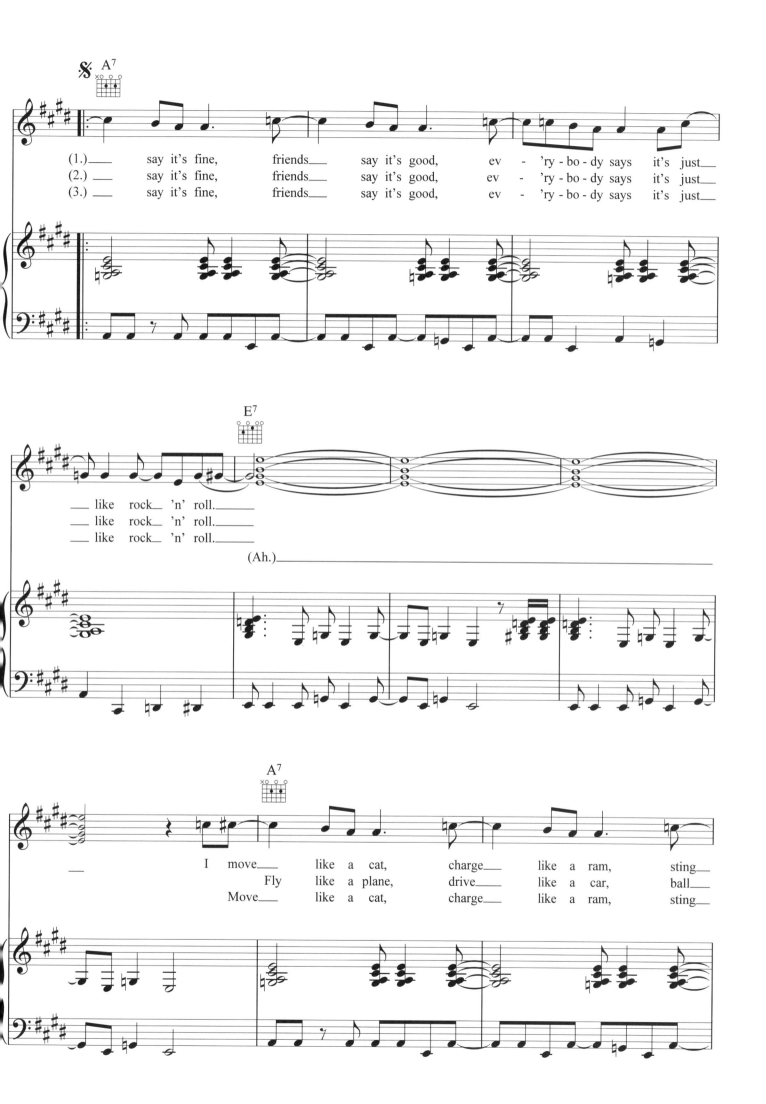

Repeat to fade

Cold As Ice

Words & Music by Mick Jones & Lou Gramm

Are You Gonna Go My Way

Words & Music by Lenny Kravitz & Craig Ross

1. I was born_____ long a - go, I'm the cho - sen, I'm the
2. I don't know why_____ we al - ways cry, this we must leave and get un -

one.
- done.   I have come   to save the day,
We must en - gage   and re - ar - range,

and I won't leave un - til I'm done.   So that's why
and turn this pla - net back to one.   So tell me why

G7

you've got to try,   you got to breath and have some fun.
we've got to die,   and kill each oth - er one by one.

G

Though I'm not paid   I play this game,   and I won't stop un - til I'm
We've got to hug   and rub - a - dub,   we've got to dance and be in

Em7

- ta   know._____

(Guitar solo)

Dream On

Words & Music by Steven Tyler

1. Ev-'ry - time____ that I look in the mir - ror all these lines____ in my

Yeah:

Sing with me, sing for the year,_ sing_ for the laugh-ter, sing_____ for the tear,_____

sing_ with me if it's just for to-day,_ may-be to-mor-row the good Lord will take you a-way.___

Hard To Handle

Words & Music by Otis Redding, Alvertis Isbell & Allen Jones

-ta come home with me._____ I have got___ some good___ old lov - in' and I

got some more in store,___ when I get___ through throw - in' it on___ you, you got___

F#7

___ to come back for more._____ { Boys and things that come___ by the do- zen, }
{ Boys come along, a dime___ by the do- zen, }

B7

N.C.

that ain't no - thin' but drug store lov - in', hey lit - tle thing let me light your can - dle 'cos a -

ma - ma, I'm sure hard to han - dle now, yes, I am.

2. Ac - tions___ speak loud - er than words,___ and I'm a

man of great ex - pe - rience,   I know you got an - oth - er man___ but I can

love you bet - ter than him.___   Take___ my hand,___ don't___ be a - fraid, I'm gon - na

The Joker

Words & Music by Steve Miller, Eddie Curtis & Ahmet Ertegun

right here, right here, right here, right here at home.___
Ooh-wee, baby, I should show you a good time. }
'Cos I'm a

pick - er, I'm a grin -ner, I'm a lov - er, and I'm a sin - ner. I play my mu-sic in the

(𝄋) *Instrumental*

sun._____ I'm a jok - er, I'm a smok - er, I'm a mid - night tok - er.

1, 3.
{ I get my lov-ing on_the run.
{ I sure don't want to hurt no -

3°D.C. to fade **2.** *D.S.*

Ooh._____

Ooh._____ - one._____

37

Maggie May

Words & Music by Rod Stewart & Martin Quittenton

1. Wake up Mag-gie, I think I've got some-thing to say to you.
(2.) morn-ing sun, when it's in your face real-ly shows your age.
3. All I need-ed was a friend to lend a guid-ing hand.

It's late Sep - tem - ber and I real - ly should be back_
But that don't wor - ry me none,__ in my eyes you're
But you turned in - to a lov - er and mo - ther, what a lov - er, you wore

_ at__ school.
ev - 'ry - thing.
me out.

I know I keep you a - mused_
I laugh at all of your jokes,__
All__ you did was wreck my bed,

but I feel I'm be - ing used.__
my love___ you did - n't need to coax.
and in the morning, kick me in the head.__

Oh,

Mag-gie, I wish I'd nev - er seen_ your face.

Rebel Yell

Words & Music by Billy Idol & Steve Stevens

I walked the walls_____ for you____ babe,_

a thou-sand miles for you.___

I dried your tears of pain,

a mil-lion times for you.___

Bm

I'd sell my soul, for you babe,_

more.

Ooh, yeah,____ lit - tle ba - by,
Ooh, yeah,____ lit - tle an - gel,

she want more,

more, more, more, more,

more.____

Saturday Night's Alright
For Fighting

Words & Music by Elton John & Bernie Taupin

1. It's get - ting__ late,__ I have -n't seen my mates,__ Ma,
(2.) pret - ty__ tight__ in__ here__ to - night, I'm looking for a

tell me when the boys get here.__ It's sev - en o'-clock and I wan-
dol - ly who will see me right.__ I may use a lit - tle mus - cle to get

- na rock,___ wan - na get___ a bel - ly - ful of beer.___ My
what I need, I may sink a lit-tle drink___ and shout out "She's with me!"___ A

old man is drunk - er than a bar - rel full of monk - eys, and my old la - dy; she don't care.
cou - ple of the sounds I real - ly like___ are the sounds___ of a switch - blade and a mo - tor - bike,

___ My sis - ter looks cute in her bra - ces and boots,___ a
___ I'm a ju - ve - nile pro - duct of the work - ing___ class___ whose best friend

hand - ful of grease__ in her hair.___)
floats in the bot - tom of a glass.___)

Don't give us none of your ag - gra - va - tion, we had it with your dis - ci - pline.

Sa - tur - day night's al - right for fight - ing, get

a lit - tle ac - tion in. Get a - bout as oiled as a

die - sel train, gon - na set this dance a - light. Sa-

56

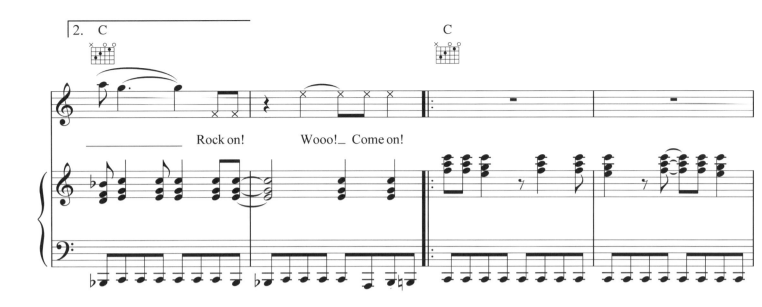

Rock on!   Wooo!_ Come on!

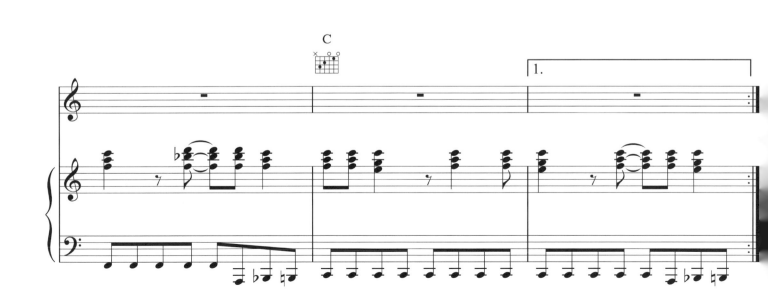

Stuck In The Middle With You

Words & Music by Gerry Rafferty & Joe Egan

1, 5.Well, I don't
3. I'm try'n'

(1, 5.) ___ know why I came here to-night, ___ I got the feel-ing that some-thing ain't right,
(2.) ___ stuck in the mid-dle with you, ___ and I'm won - d'ring what it is I should do.
(3.) ___ to make some sense of it all, ___ I can see ___ that it makes no sense at all.

(4° Instrumental)

lake a big impression with these song collections for auditions...

Audition Songs for Male Singers

Tonight...
plus All Good Gifts; Anthem; Being Alive; Corner Of The Sky; Funny;
High Flying, Adored; If I Loved You; Luck Be A Lady;
Why, God, Why? ORDER NO. AM92586

Maria...
plus All I Need Is The Girl; Bring Him Home; Frederick's Aria;
I Don't Remember Christmas; Sit Down, You're Rocking The Boat;
Some Enchanted Evening; This Is The Moment; Where I Want To Be;
You're Nothing Without Me. ORDER NO. AM950213

Angels...
Come What May; Is You Is Or Is You Ain't My Baby?; The Music Of The Night;
No Matter What; Reet Petite; Shoes Upon The Table; This Year's Love;
Try A Little Tenderness; Your Song. ORDER NO. AM972400

Perfect Day...
plus Can You Feel The Love Tonight; Can't Take My Eyes Off You;
Flying Without Wings; The Great Pretender; I Can't Make You Love Me;
I Drove All Night; Let Me Entertain You; Light My Fire;
A Little Less Conversation; Trouble. ORDER NO. AM976085

R & B Anthems...
Brown Sugar; Frontin'; Hey Ya!; Hot In Herre; Kiss;
Like I Love You; No Diggity; Rock With You;
She's got That Vibe; Yeah!. ORDER NO. AM91979

Special double-CD compilation...
lition Songs for Professional Singers
Features 28 big chart hits for men (160pp). ORDER NO. AM84708

Audition Songs for Male & Female Singers

Gilbert & Sullivan
I Am The Very Model Of A Modern Major-General; I'm Called Little Buttercup;
The Nightmare Song (When You're Lying Awake With A Dismal Headache);
On A Tree By A River (Wilow, Tit Willow); Poor Wand'ring One!;
Silvered Is The Raven Hair; The Sun Whose Rays Are All Ablaze;
Take A Pair Of Sparkling Eyes; When All Night A Chap Remains;
When Maiden Loves She Sits And Sighs. ORDER NO. AM958188

Christmas Hits
Fairytale Of New York; Happy Xmas (War Is Over);
I Wish It Could Be Christmas Every Day; Last Christmas; Lonely This Christmas;
Merry Xmas Everybody; Mistletoe And Wine; A Spaceman Came Travelling;
Step Into Christmas; Wonderful Christmastime. ORDER NO. AM971586

Christmas Ballads
Baby, It's Cold Outside; Blue Christmas; C.H.R.I.S.T.M.A.S.;
The Christmas Song (Chestnuts Roasting On An Open Fire);
The Christmas Waltz; Home For The Holidays;
I Saw Mommy Kissing Santa Claus;
Let It Snow! Let It Snow! Let It Snow!;
Santa Baby. ORDER NO. AM85465

Audition Songs for Kids
Any Dream Will Do; Consider Yourself; I'd Do Anything; No Matter What;
Spice Up Your Life; Thank You For The Music; The Candy Man; Tomorrow;
When I'm Sixty Four. ORDER NO. AM955273

More Audition Songs for Kids
The Bare Necessities; Can You Feel The Love Tonight; Food, Glorious Food;
Happy Talk; I Have A Dream; Maybe; Reach; Starlight Express; What If;
You've Got A Friend In Me. ORDER NO. AM966636

...PLUS MANY MORE
For full range of titles in the series, contact your local music retailer,
visit www.musicsales.com or email marketing@musicsales.co.uk

CD Track Listing

CD Track 1
20th Century Boy
Music: Page 4
(BOLAN) WIZARD (BAHAMAS LIMITED)

CD Track 2
Cold As Ice
Music: Page 9
(JONES/GRAMM) WARNER BROTHERS MUSIC LIMITED

CD Track 3
Are You Gonna Go My Way
Music: Page 14
(KRAVITZ/ROSS) EMI VIRGIN MUSIC LIMITED/WARNER/CHAPPELL MUSIC LIMITED

CD Track 4
Dream On
Music: Page 20
(TYLER) SONY/ATV MUSIC PUBLISHING (UK) LIMITED

CD Track 5
Hard To Handle
Music: Page 28
(REDDING/ISBELL/JONES) CARLIN MUSIC CORPORATION

CD Track 6
The Joker
Music: Page 35
(MILLER/CURTIS/ERTEGUN) WINDSWEPT MUSIC (LONDON) LIMITED

CD Track 7
Maggie May
Music: Page 38
(STEWART/QUITTENTON) EMI MUSIC PUBLISHING (WP) LIMITED/
EMI MUSIC PUBLISHING LIMITED/WARNER/CHAPPELL MUSIC LIMITED

CD Track 8
Rebel Yell
Music: Page 45
(IDOL/STEVENS) CHRYSALIS MUSIC LIMITED/WARNER/CHAPPELL MUSIC LIMITED

CD Track 9
Saturday Night's Alright For Fighting
Music: Page 54
(JOHN/TAUPIN) UNIVERSAL/DICK JAMES MUSIC LIMITED

CD Track 10
Stuck In The Middle With You
Music: Page 60
(RAFFERTY/EGAN) UNIVERSAL MUSIC PUBLISHING/BABY BUN MUSIC LIMITED

SECTION 3
CLASSICAL GREATS

Notes And Original Texts

Songs are listed alphabetically by title

Dates indicate the first performance of each work

AVE MARIA

1859

Composed by Charles Gounod

Ave Maria, gratia plena,
Dominus tecum benedictatus in mulieribus.
Et benedictus fructus ventris tui Jésus,
Sancta Maria, sancta Maria, Maria,
Ora pro nobis, nobis peccatoribus.
Nunc et in hora, in hora mortis nostrae,
Amen! Amen!

RECORDINGS

José Carreras on *Ave Maria*, Universal International Music B.V. (1984)
Daniel Rodriguez on *The Spirit Of America*, EMI-Manhattan (2002)
Bryn Terfel on *Simple Gifts*, Deutsche Grammophon (2005)

CHE FARÒ SENZA EURIDICE (from 'ORFEO ED EURIDICE')

1762

Music by Christoph Willibald Gluck
Libretto by Ranieri Calzabigi

Che farò senza Euridice?
Dove andrò senza il mio ben?
Che farò? Dove andrò?
Che farò senza il mio ben?
Euridice! Euridice!
Oh Dio! Rispondi, rispondi!
Io son pure il tuo fedele,
Che farò senza Euridice?
Ah! Non m'avanza più soccorso,
Più speranza nè dal mondo.
Nè dal ciel!
Che farò senza Euridice?

RECORDINGS

Dietrich Fischer-Dieskau on *Gluck: Orfeo Ed Euridice*, Deutsche Grammophon (1993)
Luciano Pavarotti on *O Holy Night*, Decca Music Group Limited (2005)

DEH, VIENI ALLA FINESTRA (from 'DON GIOVANNI')
1787
Music by Wolfgang Amadeus Mozart
Libretto by Lorenzo Da Ponte

Deh, vieni alla finestra, o mio tesoro. Deh, vieni a consolar il pianto mio.
Se neghi a me di dar qualche ristoro, davanti agli occhi tuoi morir vogl'io!
Tu ch'hai la bocca dolce più che il miele tu che il zucchero porti in mezzo al core!
Non esser, gioia mia, con me crudele! Lasciati almen veder, mio bell'amore!

RECORDINGS
Dietrich Fischer-Dieskau on *Don Giovanni*, Deutsche Grammophon (1990)
Bryn Terfel on *Bryn Terfel: Opera Arias*, Deutsche Grammophon (1996)

ERLKÖNIG
1815
Music by Franz Schubert
Poem by Johann Wolfgang Von Goethe

Wer reitet so spät durch Nacht und Wind? Es ist der Vater mit seinem Kind;
Er hält den Knaben wohl in dem Arm, er hält ihn sicher, er hält ihn warm.

"Mein Sohn, was birgst du so scheu dein Gesicht?"
"Siehst, Vater, du den Erlkönig nicht? Den Erlenkönig mit Kron und Schweif?"
"Mein Sohn, es ist ein Nebelstreif."

"Du liebes Kind, komm, geh mit mir! Gar schöne Spiele spiel ich mit dir;
Manch bunte Blumen sind an dem Strand, Meine Mutter hat manch gülden Gewand."

"Mein Vater, mein Vater, und hörest du nicht, was Erlenkönig mir heimlich verspricht?"
"Sei ruhig, bleibe ruhig, mein Kind: In dürren Blättern säuselt der Wind."

"Willst, feiner Knabe, du mit mir gehn? Meine Töchter sollen dich warten schön;
 Meine Töchter führen den nächtlichen Reihn. Und wiegen und tanzen und singen dich ein."

"Mein Vater, mein Vater, und siehst du nicht dort, Erlkönigs Töchter am düstern Ort?"
"Mein Sohn, mein Sohn, ich seh es genau: es scheinen die alten Weiden so grau."

"Ich liebe dich, mich reizt deine schöne Gestalt; und bist du nicht willig, so brauch ich Gewalt."
"Mein Vater, mein Vater, jetzt fasst er mich an! Erlkönig hat mir ein Leids getan!"

Dem Vater grauset's, er reitet geschwind. Er hält in Armen das ächzende Kind,
Erreicht den Hof mit Müh' und Not: In seinen Armen das Kind war tot.

RECORDINGS
Dietrich Fischer-Dieskau on *Schubert: 21 Lieder*, Angel Classics (1988)
Ian Bostridge on *Schubert: Lieder*, EMI Classics (1998)

THE FLOWER SONG (from 'CARMEN')
1875
Music by Georges Bizet
Libretto by Henri Meilhac and Ludovic Halévy

La fleur que tu m'avais jetée, dans ma prison m'était restée.
Flétrie et sèche, cette fleur Gardait toujours sa douce odeur;
Et pendant des heures entières, sur mes yeux, fermant mes paupières,
De cette odeur je m'enivrais et dans la nuit je te voyais!
Je me prenais à te maudire, a te détester, à me dire:
Pourquoi faut-il que le destin l'ait mise là sur mon chemin!
Puis je m'accusais de blasphème, et je ne sentais en moi-même,
Je ne sentais qu'un seul désir, un seul désir, un seul espoir:
Te revoir, ô Carmen, oui, te revoir! Car tu n'avais eu qu'à paraître,
Qu'à jeter un regard sur moi, pour t'emparer de tout mon être,
Ô ma Carmen! Et j'étais une chose à toi!
Carmen, je t'aime!

RECORDINGS
Plácido Domingo on *Plácido Domingo: Artist Portrait*, Teldec Classics International (2004)
Andrea Bocelli on *Andrea Bocelli: Aria: The Opera Album*, Decca Music Group (2005)

IT WAS A LOVER AND HIS LASS
1600
Music by Thomas Morley
Text by William Shakespeare

It was a lover and his lass, with a hey, and a ho, and a hey nonino,
That o'er the green corn-field did pass. In the spring time, the only pretty ring time,
When birds do sing, hey, ding-a-ding-a-ding. Sweet lovers love the spring.

Between the acres of the rye, with a hey, and a ho, and a hey nonino,
These pretty country folks did lie. In the spring time, the only pretty ring time,
When birds do sing, hey, ding-a-ding-a-ding. Sweet lovers love the spring.

This carol they began that hour, with a hey, and a ho, and a hey nonino,
How that life was but a flow'r. In the spring time, the only pretty ring time,
When birds do sing, hey, ding-a-ding-a-ding. Sweet lovers love the spring.

Then, pretty lovers, take the time, with a hey, and a ho, and a hey nonino,
For love is crowned with the prime. In the spring time, the only pretty ring time,
When birds do sing, hey, ding-a-ding-a-ding. Sweet lovers love the spring.

RECORDINGS
Bryn Terfel on *The Vagabond*, Deutsche Grammophon (1995)
Alfred Deller on *The Very Best Of English Song*, EMI (2003)

LA DONNA E MOBILE (from 'RIGOLETTO')

1851

Music by Giuseppe Verdi
Libretto by Francesco Maria Piave

La donna è mobile qual piuma al vento,
Muta d'accento e di pensiero.
Sempre un amabile leggiadro viso,
In pianto o in riso, è menzognero.
La donna è mobil, qual piùma al vento,
Muta d'accento, e di pensier e di pensier, e, e di pensier.

È sempre misero, chi a lei s'affida,
Chi le confida, mal cauto il core!
Pur mai non sentesi felice appieno
Chi su quel seno non liba amore!
La donna è mobil, qual piuma al vento,
Muta d'accento e di pensier,
E di pensier, e, e di pensier!

RECORDINGS

Russell Watson on *Russell Watson: The Voice*, Decca Music Group Ltd. (2000)
Andrea Bocelli on *Andrea Bocelli: Aria: The Opera Album*, Decca Music Group (2005)

O FOR THE WINGS OF A DOVE

1844

Music by Felix Mendelssohn
Words by William Bartholomew

O for the wings of a dove!
Far away would I rove!
O for the wings, for the wings of a dove!
Far away, far away, far away, far away would I rove!
In the wilderness build me a nest and remain there forever at rest,
In the wilderness build me a nest and remain there forever at rest,
In the wilderness build me a nest. Remain there forever at rest,
And remain there forever at rest, and remain there forever at rest.
And remain there forever at rest, forever at rest, forever at rest,
And remain there forever at rest, and remain there forever at rest.

RECORDINGS

Aled Jones on *New Horizons*, Universal Classics & Jazz (2005)

UNA FURTIVA LAGRIMA (from 'L'ELISIR D'AMORE')

1832
Music by Gaetano Donizetti
Libretto by Felice Romani

Una furtiva lagrima
Negl'occhi suoi spuntò:
Quelle festose giovani
Invidiar sembrò:
Che più cercando io vo?
M'ama, lo vedo.
Un solo istante i palpiti
Del suo bel cor sentir!
I miei sospir confondere
Per poco a'suoi sospir!
I palpiti i palpiti sentir!
Confondere i miei co'suoi sospir!
Cielo, si può morir;
Di più non chiedo.

RECORDINGS

Plácido Domino on *Plácido Domingo: Greatist Hits*, Classics/Windham (1994)
Luciano Pavarotti on *The 3 Tenors*, X5 Music Group (2005)

WIEGENLIED

1868
Music by Johannes Brahms
Text by Karl Simrock

Guten Abend, gut' Nacht, mit Rosen bedacht,
Mit Näglein besteckt, schlupf unter die Deck'
Morgen früh, wenn Gott will, wirst du wieder geweckt,
Morgen früh, wenn Gott will, wirst du wieder geweckt.

Guten Abend, gute Nacht, von Englein bewacht,
Die zeigen im Traum, dir Christkindleins Baum;
Schlaf nun selig und süss, schau im Traum's Paradies,
Schlaf nun selig und süss, schau im Traum's Paradies.

RECORDINGS

Plácido Domingo on *A Tenor's Christmas*, Sony Classical (1997)
Bryn Terfel on *Bryn Terfel Sings Favourites*, Deutsche Grammophon (2003)

Ave Maria

Composed by Charles Gounod

Che Farò Senza Euridice

(from 'Orfeo Ed Euridice')

Music by Christoph Willibald Gluck
Libretto by Ranieri Calzabigi

Allegretto

Che fa - rò sen - za Eu - ri - di - ce? Do - ve an - drò sen - za il mio

ben? Che fa - rò?___ Do - ve an - drò?___ Che fa -

-rò___ sen - za il mi - o ben? Do - ve an - drò___ sen - za il mi - o

ben? Eu - ri - di - ce! Eu - ri -

- di - ce! Oh Di - o! Ri - spon - di,

ri - spon - - - - di! I - o son___

Adagio

p col canto

* When singing to the CD backing track, hold this note for 3 counts.

pu - re il tu - o fe - de - le, io son pu - re il tu - o fe -

Tempo 1

- de - le, il tu - o fe - de - le, Che fa - rò sen - za Eu - ri -

- di - ce? Do-ve an - drò sen-za il mio ben? Che fa -

- rò?_____ Do - ve an - drò?_____ Che__ fa - rò__ sen - za il mi - o

f

ben? Do - ve an - drò___ sen - za il mi - o ben? Eu - ri - di - ce! Eu - ri -

Adagio

- di - ce! Ah! Non m'a - van - za più___ soc - cor - so, più___ spe -

Tempo 1

- ran - za nè dal mon - do. nè___ dal ciel! Che fa -

- rò sen - za E - u - ri - di - ce? Do - ve an - drò sen - za il mio ben? Che_ fa -

_f_

- rò?_____ Do - ve an - drò?_____ Che_ fa - rò_ sen - za il mi - o

ben? Do - ve an - drò?_____ Che_ fa - rò?_____ Do - ve an -

- drò_ sen - za il mi - o ben?

18

Deh, Vieni Alla Finestra
(from 'Don Giovanni')
Music by Wolfgang Amadeus Mozart
Libretto by Lorenzo Da Ponte

Alegretto

Deh,

vie - ni_al - la fi - ne - stra, o mi - o te - so - ro. Deh,

vie - ni_a con - so - lar il pian - to mi - o.

Se ne - ghi_a me___ di dar qual - -che ri - sto - ro, da - van ti_a - gli_oc - chi tuoi mo - - rir___ vo - gl'i - o.

Tu ch'hai___ la boc - ca dol - ce più_____ che il mie - le

20

tu che_il zuc-che-ro por - ti in mez - zo_al co - re!

Non es - ser, gio - ia mia, con

me cru-de - le! La - scia-ti_al-men__ ve - der, mio

bell'___ a - mo - re!

Erlkönig

Music by Franz Schubert
Poem by Johann Wolfgang Von Goethe

Wer rei - tet so spät   durch Nacht und

Wind?

Es ist der Va - ter mit

sei - nem Kind; er hält den Knab - en

wohl in dem Arm, er hält ihn sich - er, er

hält ihn warm.

f

dir; manch bunt - - e Blu - men sind

an dem Strand, mein - e Mut - ter hat manch

gül - - den Ge - wand." "Mein Va - ter, mein

Va - ter, und hö - rest du nicht, was Er - len - kö - nig mir

heim - lich ver - spricht?"   "Sei

ru - hig,   bleib - e ru - hig, mein Kind: In dür - ren

Blät - tern säu - selt der Wind."   "Willst,

fei - ner__ Knab - e, du mit mir gehn? Mei - ne Töch - ter sol - len dich

dim.

ppp

27

war - ten schön; mei - ne Töch - ter— führ - en den nächt - lich - en Reihn. Und

wie - gen und tan - zen und sin - gen dich ein, und wie - gen und tan - zen und

sin - gen dich ein." "Mein Va - ter, mein Va - ter, und

siehst du nicht dort, Erl - kö - nigs Töch - ter am düst - ern

Ort?"   "Mein   Sohn,   mein   Sohn,   ich

seh   es   ge - nau: Es   schei - nen die al - ten   Wei - den   so

grau."

"Ich   lie -   be dich,   mich   reizt   dei - ne schö - ne Ges -

-talt; und bist du nicht wil - lig, so brauch ich Ge-

-walt." "Mein Va - ter, mein Va - ter, jetzt fasst er mich

an! Erl - kö - nig hat mir ein Leids ge -

-tan!" Dem Va - ter grau - set's, er

rei - tet gesch- wind, Er hält in Arm - en das

cresc.

äch - zen - de Kind, er -

ff

- reicht den Hof mit Müh' und Not:

ff *f* *fp*

Recit.   **Andante**

in sei-nem Arm - en das Kind war tot.

pp *p* *f*

The Flower Song
(from 'Carmen')

Music by Georges Bizet
Libretto by Henri Meilhac and Ludovic Halévy

Performance Note: The cadenza bars have been fixed into strict tempi to make CD-accompanied performances easier.

- deur; et pen - dant des heu - res en - tiè - res, sur mes

yeux, fer-mant mes pau - piè - res, de cet - te o - deur je m'en i -

-vrais et dans la nuit je te vo - yais! Je

Poco animato, ma poco *cresc.*

me pre - nais à te mau - di - re, a te dé - tes - ter, à me

di - re: Pour - quoi faut - il___ que le des - tin l'ait___ mi - se

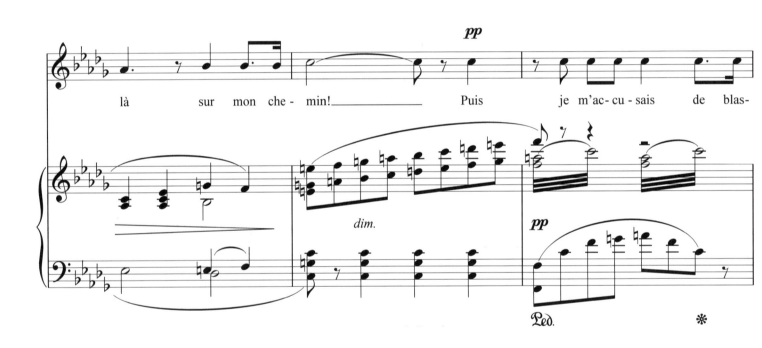

là sur mon che - min!_____ Puis je m'ac-cu-sais de blas-

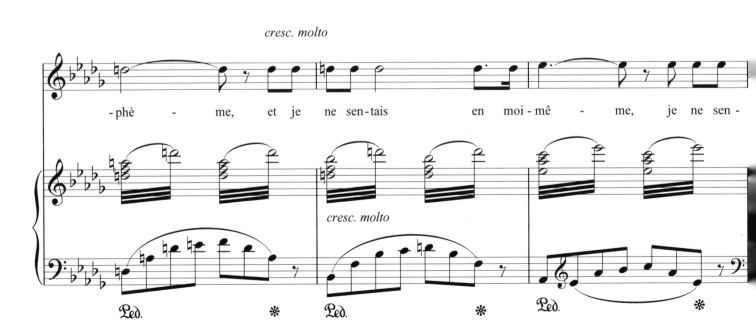

-phè - me, et je ne sen-tais en moi-mê - me, je ne sen-

moi, pour t'em-pa - rer de tout mon ê - tre, ô ma Car-men!

Et j'é - tais une cho-se à toi!_____

Car - men, je

t'ai - - - - me!

It Was A Lover And His Lass

Music by Thomas Morley
Text by William Shakespeare

spring - time, in spring - time, in spring - time, the

on - ly pret - ty ring - time, when birds do sing, hey,

ding - a - ding - a - ding, hey, ding - a - ding - a - ding, hey,

ding - a - ding - a - ding. Sweet lov - ers love the spring! In spring -

-time, in spring - time, the on - ly
pret - ty ring - time, when birds do sing, hey,
ding - a - ding - a - ding, hey, ding - a - ding - a - ding, hey, ding - a - ding - a - ding, sweet

1-3. **4**

lov - ers love the spring.

2. Be -
3. This spring.
4. Then,

La Donna E Mobile
(from 'Rigoletto')

Music by Giuseppe Verdi
Libretto by Francesco Maria Piave

Performance Note: The cadenza bars have been fixed into strict tempi to make CD-accompanied performances easier.

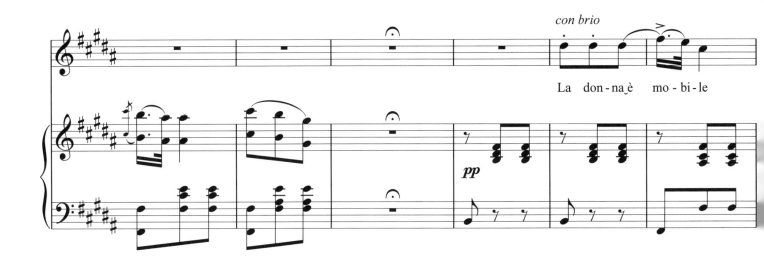

Sem-pre un a - ma-bi-le   leg-gia-dro   vi-so,   in   pian-to o in   ri - so,

è   men-zo - gne-ro.   La___   don-na e   mo - bil   qual___ più-ma al   ven - to,

mu - ta d'ac - cen - to___   e___ di   pen - sier,

e___   di   pen - sier,   e,_____

con forza

e___ di___ pen - sier.

ff

p marcato

È sem - pre

pp

mi - se - ro chi a lei s'af - fi - da, chi le con - fi - da mal cau - to il

p

pp

co - re! Pur mai non sen - te - si fe li - ce ap - pie - no chi su quel

pp

pp

se____ no non li - ba_a - mo - re! La____ don-na_è mo - bil qual__ piu-me_al

ven - to, mu - ta d'ac - cen - to____ e__ di pen - sier,

e____ di pen - sier, e,_____

e____ di__ pen - sier!

O For The Wings Of A Dove

Music by Felix Mendelssohn
Words by William Bartholomew

Con moto

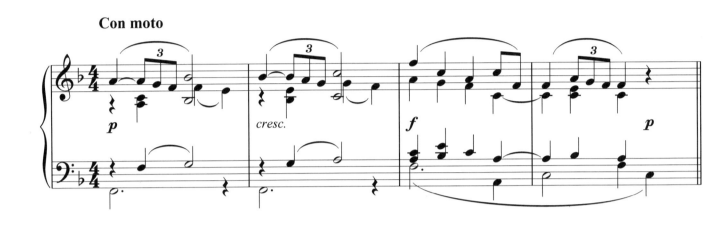

O_____ for the wings,___ for the wings___ of a dove! Far a - way, far a-

-way would I rove! O_____ for the wings,___ for the wings___ of a dove!

in_____ the wil - der-ness build me a nest.____ And re - main there for -

-ev - er at rest, and_____ re - main_____ there for - ev - er at rest,

and_____ re - main_____ there for - ev - - - er at rest.

And re - main there for - ev - er at rest, for - ev - er at rest,

for - ev - - - - - - - - - er   at

rest,   and____ re - main____ there for - ev - - er at rest,

and____ re - main____ there for - ev - - - - er   at

p

rest._____

pp

Una Furtiva Lagrima
(from 'L'Elisir D'Amore')

Music by Gaetano Donizetti
Libretto by Felice Romani

Performance Note: The cadenza bars have been fixed into strict tempi to make CD-accompanied performances easier.

Larghetto

U - na fur - ti - va la - gri - ma_____ neg - l'oc - chi suoi___ spun -

-tò: quel - le fe - sto - se gio - va-ni in -

-vi - di - ar___ sem - brò: che più cer - can - do io

vo? Che più cer - can - do io vo?

M'a - ma, sì m'a - ma,___ lo ve - do, lo ve -

49

-do. Un so - lo i - stan - te i pal - pi - ti del suo bel cor___ sen - tir!

I miei so - spir con - fon - de - re per po-co a' suoi_ so-spir! I

pal - pi-ti i pal - pi-ti sen - tir! Con - fon - de-re i mi-ei co' suoi so-

-spir!   Cie - lo,   si   può___   mo - rir;   di___ più___ non___

chie - do, non chie - do,   ah!   Cie - lo,   si   può, si può_ mo -

poco rit.

-rir;   di più___ non chie-do non chie - - - - - -

a tempo

-do.

Wiegenlied

Music by Johannes Brahms
Text by Karl Simrock

With gentle motion *(Zart bewegt)*

Gu - ten A - bend, gut' Nacht, mit

Ro - sen be - dacht, mit Näg - lein be - steckt schlupf

un - ter die Deck', Mor - gen früh, wenn Gott will, wirst du

wie - der ge - weckt, mor - gen früh, wenn Gott will, wirst du

wie - der ge - weckt. Gu - ten

A - bend, gute Nacht, von Eng - lein be - wacht, die

zei - gen im___ Traum dir___ Christ - kind - leins Baum; schlaf nun

se - lig und süss, schau' im Traum's Pa - ra - dies, schlaf nun

se - lig und süss, schau' im Traum's Pa - ra - dies.

Bringing you the words and the music

All the latest music in print... rock & pop plus jazz, blues, country, classical and the best in West End show scores.

- Books to match your favourite CDs.

- Book-and-CD titles with high quality backing tracks for you to play along to. Now you can play guitar or piano with your favourite artist... or simply sing along!

- Audition songbooks with CD backing tracks for both male and female singers for all those with stars in their eyes.

- Can't read music? No problem, you can still play all the hits with our wide range of chord songbooks.

- Check out our range of instrumental tutorial titles, taking you from novice to expert in no time at all!

- Musical show scores include *The Phantom Of The Opera*, *Les Misérables*, *Mamma Mia* and many more hit productions.

- DVD master classes featuring the techniques of top artists.

CD Track Listing

To remove your CD from the plastic sleeve,
lift the small lip to break the perforations.
Replace the disc after use for convenient storage.

SECTION 4
ANGELS...
PLUS 9 MORE HIT SONGS

Angels

Words & Music by Robbie Williams & Guy Chambers

Moderately

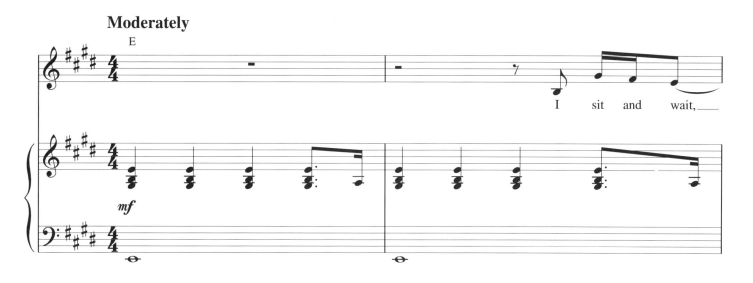

I sit and wait,___

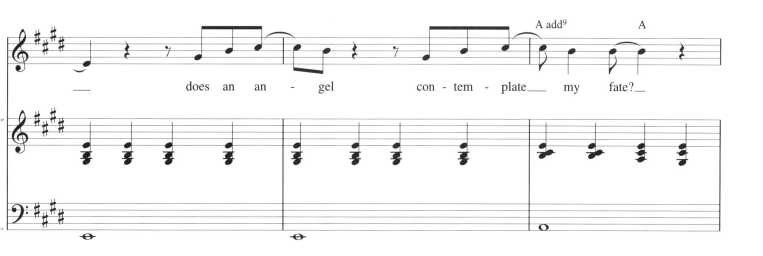

___ does an an - gel con - tem - plate___ my fate?___

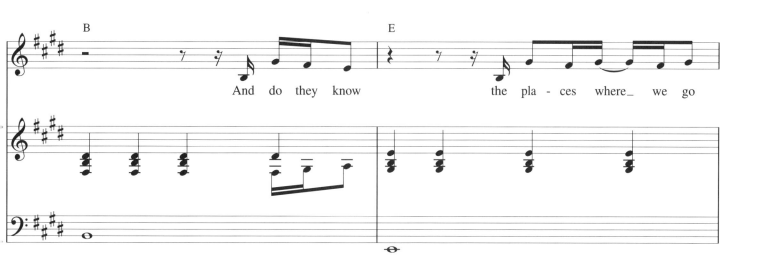

And do they know the pla - ces where_ we go

when we're grey and old?___ 'Cause I have been___

told that sal - va - tion lets their wings___ un - fold,___

So when I'm ly - ing in my bed thoughts

run - ning through my head and I feel that love is dead,___

6

8

And through it all_____ she of-fers me___ pro-tec-tion, a lot of love and af-fe

Come What May

Words & Music by David Baerwald

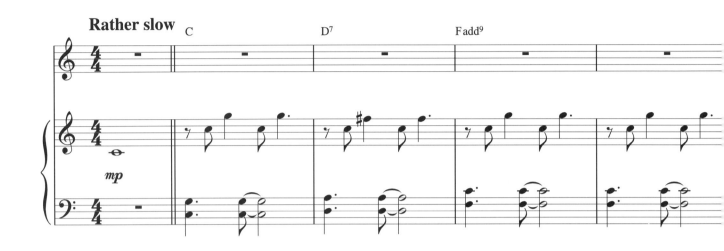

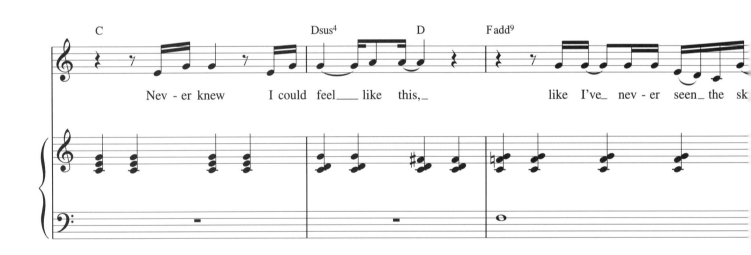

Nev - er knew I could feel___ like this,_ like I've_ nev - er seen_ the sk

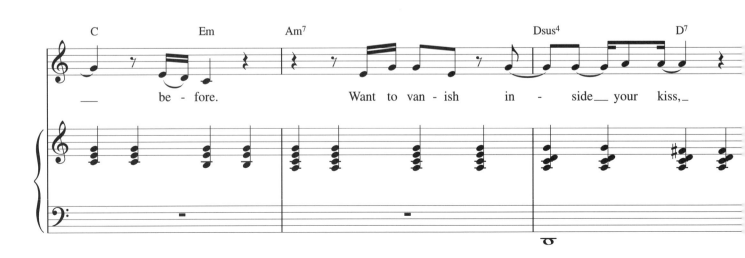

___ be - fore. Want to van - ish in - side___ your kiss,_

15

Is You Is Or Is You Ain't My Baby?

Words & Music by Billy Austin & Louis Jordan

Is you is___ or is you ain't___ my ba - by?___

May - be ba - by's found___ some - bo - dy new, ___ or

1.
is my ba - by still___ my ba - by true.___

2.
is my ba - by still___ my ba - by true.___

21

The Music Of The Night

Music by Andrew Lloyd Webber
Lyrics by Charles Hart
Additional Lyrics by Richard Stilgoe

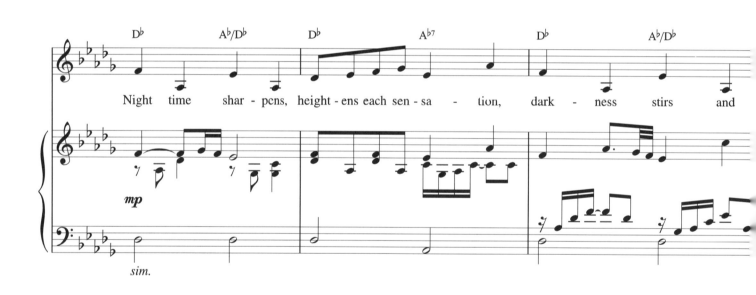

Night time shar - pens, height - ens each sen - sa - tion, dark - ness stirs and

wakes i - ma - gi - na - tion, si - lent - ly the sen - ses a

Turn your face a - way from the gar - ish light of day, turn your thoughts a - way from cold, un - feel - ing light, and list - en to the mu - sic of the night. Close your eyes and sur - ren - der to your dark - est dreams, purge your thoughts of the life you knew be

be. On - ly then can you be - long to me.

Float - ing, fall - ing, sweet in - tox - i - ca - tion, touch me, trust me,

sa - vour each sen - sa - tion, let the dream be - gin, let your dark - er side give in to the

pow - er of the mu - sic that I write, the pow - er of the mu - sic of the

No Matter What

Music by Andrew Lloyd Webber
Words by Jim Steinman

Gentle beat

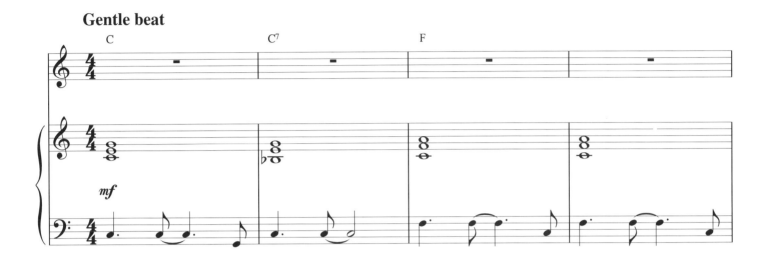

No mat - ter what they tell us,
(Verse 2 see block lyric)

no mat - ter what they do,

I know our love's for - ev - er, I know no mat - ter what.

No mat - ter who they fol - low, no mat - ter where they

Verse 2:
If only tears were laughter, if only night were day,
If only prayers were answered, then we would hear God say.
No matter what they tell you, no matter what they do,
No matter what they teach you, what you believe is true.
And I will keep you safe and strong and sheltered from the storm.
No matter where it's barren our dream is being born.

Reet Petite

Words & Music by Tyran Carlo & Berry Gordy Jr.

D. 𝄋 al Coda

Verse 2:
Well, she's like honey from a bee,
And like bees from a tree
I love her, need her, she beez so buzzin,
She's alright, she's got what it takes, she's got what it takes and to me she really rates
Well oh, now she's my cutey, my tutti frutti,
My heart, my love, my bathin' beauty, she's alright,
She's just got what it takes, she's got what it takes and to me she really rates.

Oh, oh, oh, oh, *etc.*

Shoes Upon The Table

Words & Music by Willy Russell

Bright 4

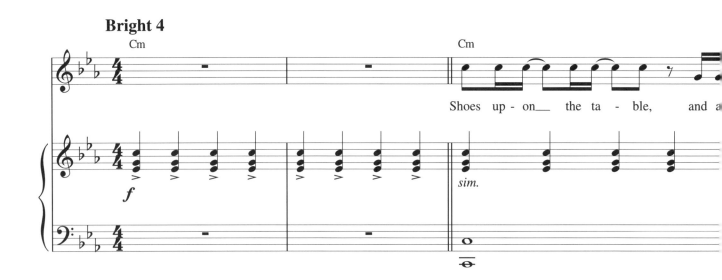

Shoes up-on__ the ta - ble, and a

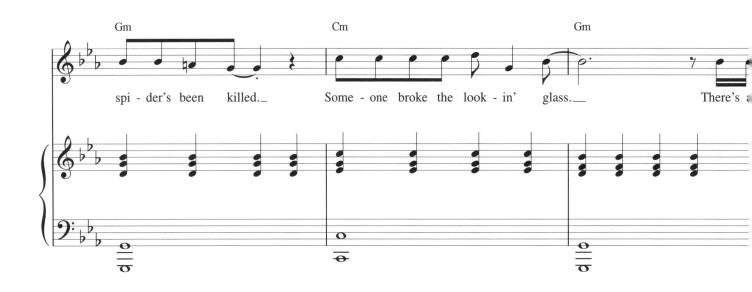

spi - der's been killed.__ Some - one broke the look - in' glass.__ There's a

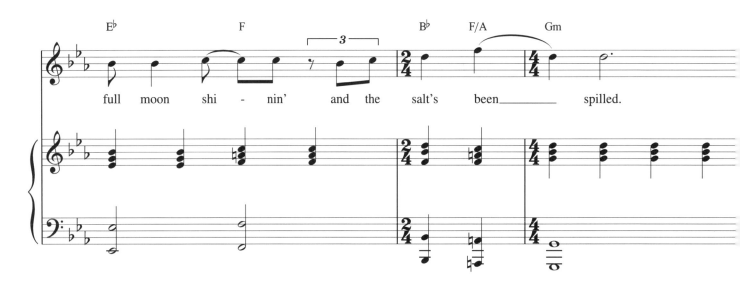

full moon shi - nin' and the salt's been__ spilled.

B♭ F/A Cm E♭
know the de - vil's got your number. You know he's gon - na find
F E♭ F E♭
you, you know he's right be - hind you, he's stan -
F D7/F♯ Cm F D7/F♯
- din' on your step and he's knock - in' at your door. He knock - in' at your door,
rall.
Cm F D7/F♯ Cm
he's knock - in' at your door.

Try A Little Tenderness

Words & Music by Harry Woods, Jimmy Campbell & Reg Connelly

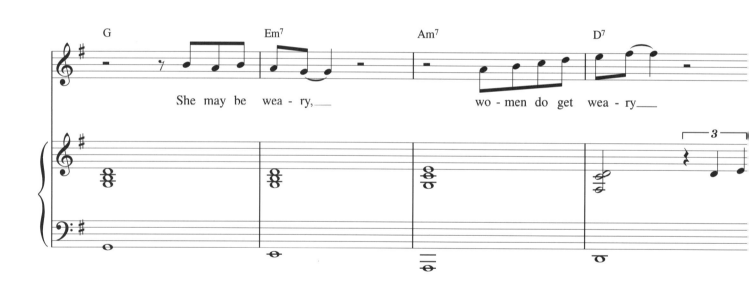

She may be wea-ry, wo-men do get wea-ry

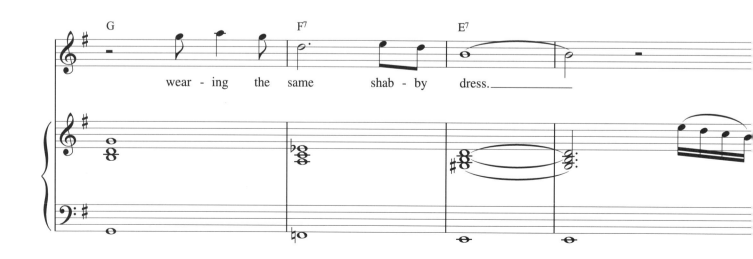

wear-ing the same shab-by dress.

More rhythmic

Your Song

Words & Music by Elton John & Bernie Taupin

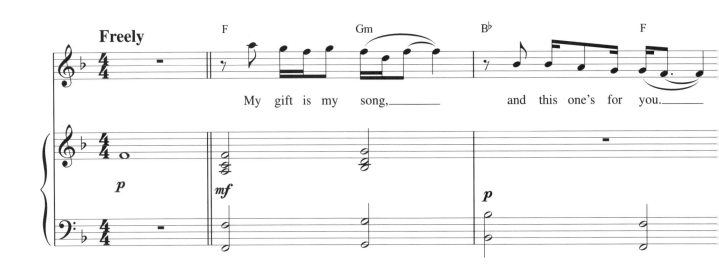

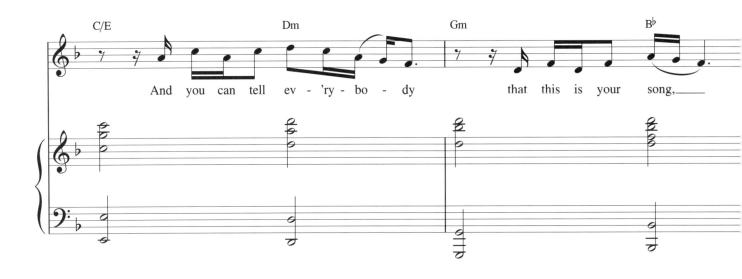

Hope you don't mind, I hope you don't mind that I put down in words how won-der-ful life_ is___ now you're_ in the world._

Sat on the roof,_ and I kicked off the moss,_____

well some of these vers-es, well_ they, they got me quite cross.___

This Year's Love

Words & Music by David Gray

Slow

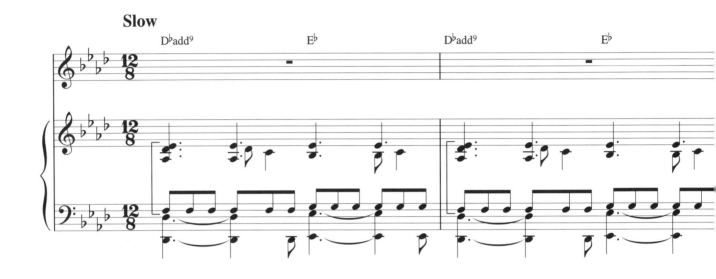

1. This year's love had bet - ter last;_____ hea - ven knows, it's high

Verse 3:
'Cause who's to worry if our hearts get torn
When that hurt gets thrown?
Don't you know this life goes on?
Won't you kiss me on that midnight street
Sweep me off my feet
Singing ain't this life so sweet?

Other great book & CD song collections for auditions...

Audition Songs for Female Singers 1
Don't Cry For Me Argentina...
plus Adelaide's Lament, Big Spender; Heaven Help My Heart;
't Say No; I Will Survive; Out Here On My Own; Saving All My Love For You;
neone To Watch Over Me; The Wind Beneath My Wings. ORDER NO. AM92587

Audition Songs for Female Singers 2
I Dreamed A Dream...
plus Another Suitcase In Another Hall; Fame; If I Were A Bell; Miss Byrd;
he Best For Last; Someone Else's Story; There Are Worse Things I Could Do;
What I Did For Love; You Can Always Count On Me. ORDER NO. AM950224

Audition Songs for Female Singers 3
Memory...
plus Can't Help Lovin' Dat Man; Crazy; Diamonds Are A Girl's Best Friend;
Now That I've Seen Her; Show Me Heaven; That Ole Devil Called Love;
The Winner Takes It All; Wishing You Were Somehow Here Again;
The Reason. ORDER NO. AM955284

Audition Songs for Female Singers 4
I Don't Know How To Love Him...
plus As Long As He Needs Me; Constant Craving; Feeling Good;
I Say A Little Prayer; If My Friends Could See Me Now;
It's Oh So Quiet; Killing Me Softly With His Song; Tell Me It's Not True;
You Must Love Me. ORDER NO. AM955295

Audition Songs for Female Singers 5
Chart Hits
st All Odds (Take A Look At Me Now); American Pie; ...Baby One More Time;
thless; It Feels So Good; Man! I Feel Like A Woman; My Love Is Your Love;
Pure Shores; Rise; Sing It Back. ORDER NO. AM963765

Audition Songs for Female Singers 6
90's Hits
History Repeating; I Will Always Love You; Never Ever; Perfect Moment;
Search For The Hero; That Don't Impress Me Much; Torn; 2 Become 1;
What Can I Do; You Gotta Be. ORDER NO. AM963776

Audition Songs for Male Singers 1
Tonight...
plus All Good Gifts; Anthem; Being Alive; Corner Of The Sky; Funny;
High Flying, Adored; If I Loved You; Luck Be A Lady;
Why, God, Why? ORDER NO. AM92586

Audition Songs for Male Singers 2
Maria...
plus All I Need Is The Girl; Bring Him Home; Frederick's Aria;
I Don't Remember Christmas; Sit Down, You're Rocking The Boat;
Some Enchanted Evening; This Is The Moment; Where I Want To Be;
You're Nothing Without Me. ORDER NO. AM950213

Audition Songs for Male & Female Singers
Gilbert & Sullivan
I Am The Very Model Of A Modern Major-General; I'm Called Little Buttercup;
The Nightmare Song (When You're Lying Awake With A Dismal Headache);
On A Tree By A River (Willow, Tit Willow); Poor Wand'ring One!;
Silvered Is The Raven Hair; The Sun Whose Rays Are All Ablaze;
Take A Pair Of Sparkling Eyes; When All Night A Chap Remains;
When Maiden Loves She Sits And Sighs. ORDER NO. AM958188

Audition Songs for Male & Female Singers
Christmas Hits
Fairytale Of New York; Happy Xmas (War Is Over);
I Wish It Could Be Christmas Every Day; Last Christmas; Lonely This Christmas;
Merry Xmas Everybody; Mistletoe And Wine; A Spaceman Came Travelling;
Step Into Christmas; Wonderful Christmastime. ORDER NO. AM971586

Audition Songs for Kids
Any Dream Will Do; Consider Yourself; I'd Do Anything; No Matter What;
Spice Up Your Life; Thank You For The Music; The Candy Man; Tomorrow;
When I'm Sixty Four. ORDER NO. AM955273

ALL TITLES AVAILABLE FROM GOOD MUSIC RETAILERS OR, IN CASE OF DIFFICULTY, CONTACT
MUSIC SALES LIMITED, NEWMARKET ROAD, BURY ST. EDMUNDS, SUFFOLK IP33 3YB
TELEPHONE: 01284 725725; FAX: 01284 702592
WWW.MUSICSALES.COM

To remove your CD from the plastic sleeve, lift the small
lip on the right to break the perforated flap.
Replace the disc after use for convenient storage.